SOAP

GAME

ANOTHER GAME

THE
BAD CHAIR

For my dad

Groundwood Books / House of Anansi Press
groundwoodbooks.com

We gratefully acknowledge the Government of Canada for its financial support of our publishing program.

With the participation of the Government of Canada
Avec la participation du gouvernement du Canada | Canada

Library and Archives Canada Cataloguing in Publication
Title: The bad chair / Dasha Tolstikova.
Names: Tolstikova, Dasha, author, illustrator.
Identifiers: Canadiana (print) 20190225297 | Canadiana (ebook) 20190225327 | ISBN 9781773062464 (hardcover) | ISBN 9781773062471 (EPUB) | ISBN 9781773064215 (Kindle)
Classification: LCC PS8639.O452 B33 2020 | DDC jC813/.6—dc23

The illustrations were created with watercolor, gouache, graphite and digital media.
Design by Michael Solomon
Printed and bound in China

FSC
www.fsc.org
MIX
Paper from
responsible sources
FSC® C144853

The Bad Chair

by Dasha Tolstikova

Groundwood Books
House of Anansi Press
Toronto Berkeley

More than anything, Chair
wanted to be in on the game.

Vivi and Monkey played the
game every night before bed.

Monkey hid under a sheet,
and Vivi pretended she
didn't know where he was.

First she looked
for him in all the
usual places.

Then she rounded up the witnesses:

Chair,

Plant,

Kettle and Cat.

"Have you seen Monkey?" she asked each of them.

Everyone stared blankly,
and eventually went back
to whatever they had
been doing.

Everyone except Chair, that is.
Chair only had eyes for Vivi.

When Vivi got tired of looking,

Monkey lifted up
his sheet and said,
"Here I am!"

And they went to get ready for bed.

But on Thursday, Chair had an idea.
If Monkey needed a bath, he would be
late for the game.

"Maybe tonight Vivi will look for
ME!" Chair thought.

Thinking the game had already started, Vivi began to look for Monkey, like she always did.

She questioned the witnesses, like she always did.

But when she got tired, Monkey did NOT lift up his sheet and say, "Here I am!"

"It's been fifteen minutes," said Vivi.
"Where is he?"

"Look!" said Chair.
"I can hide, too!"

"Look for me!"

But just as Chair really got
into the game,

Vivi said, "This is not like Monkey.
He may be in trouble. I need to look harder."

"I thought WE were playing," grumbled Chair.

But Vivi had already walked away. She would
question the witnesses again. And this time she
meant business.

The first witness Vivi came upon was Plant.
He had recently fallen in love.
"Listen!" said Vivi. "Are you SURE you
haven't seen Monkey?"
But Plant ignored her. He was busy
looking wistfully at Cat.

"Cat!" said Vivi. "Cat! What about you?
When is the last time YOU saw Monkey?"

But Cat didn't even look up. She was busy running after her toy mouse.
There was just one more witness to question.

"Kettle, did you see
Monkey, AFTER ALL?"

But Kettle was busy, too.
It was time for tea.

Vivi plopped down on Chair.
"Where can he be?" she said. She was
beginning to feel hopeless.

"I'm sure he's fine,"
said Chair. "Let's
just go back to the
living room."

"WAIT A SECOND!"
There was someone Vivi had
forgotten about.
"Chair," she said, "do YOU
know something?"

Chair looked
away shiftily.

"You DO!" yelled Vivi.
"Tell me immediately!"

"Oh FINE," said Chair. "I'll tell you ..."

And just at that moment,
Monkey came out of the laundry
room, freshly clean.
"Hey, dudes, what's going on?"
he said.

"Monkey! I am so happy to see you!" Vivi cried.

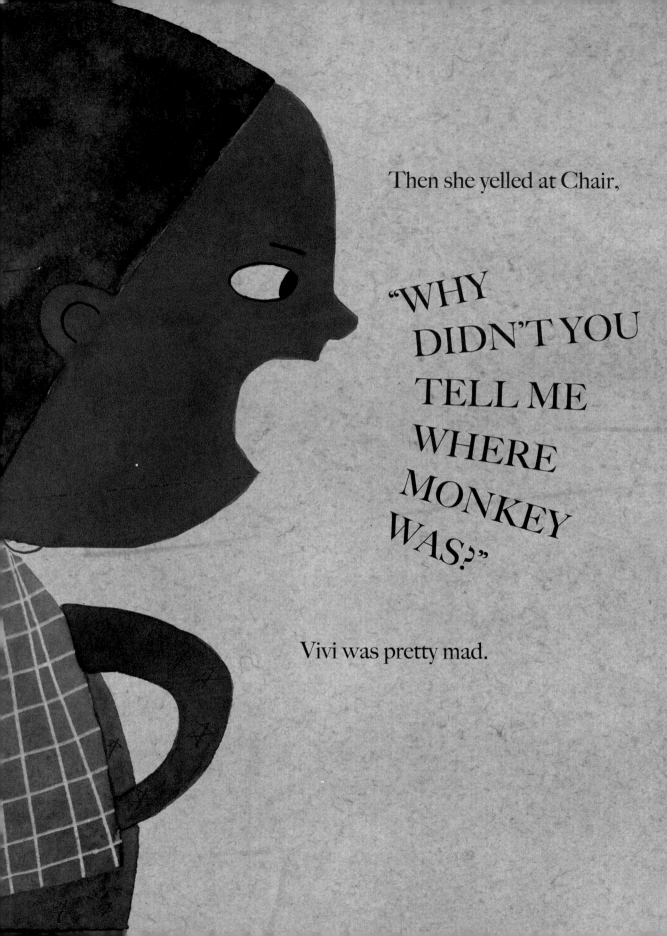

Then she yelled at Chair,

"WHY
DIDN'T YOU
TELL ME
WHERE
MONKEY
WAS?"

Vivi was pretty mad.

"I just wanted to play, too," said Chair.

"I have so much to tell you," Vivi said to Monkey as they went to get ready for bed.

"Now I will never be in on the game,"
thought Chair.

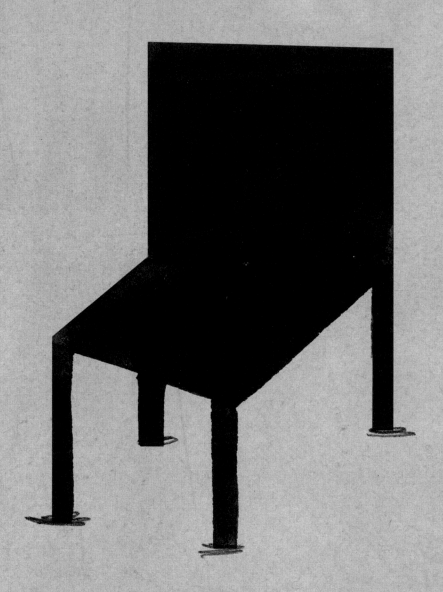

But then Vivi came out of her room and said, "Hey, tomorrow do YOU want to hide?"

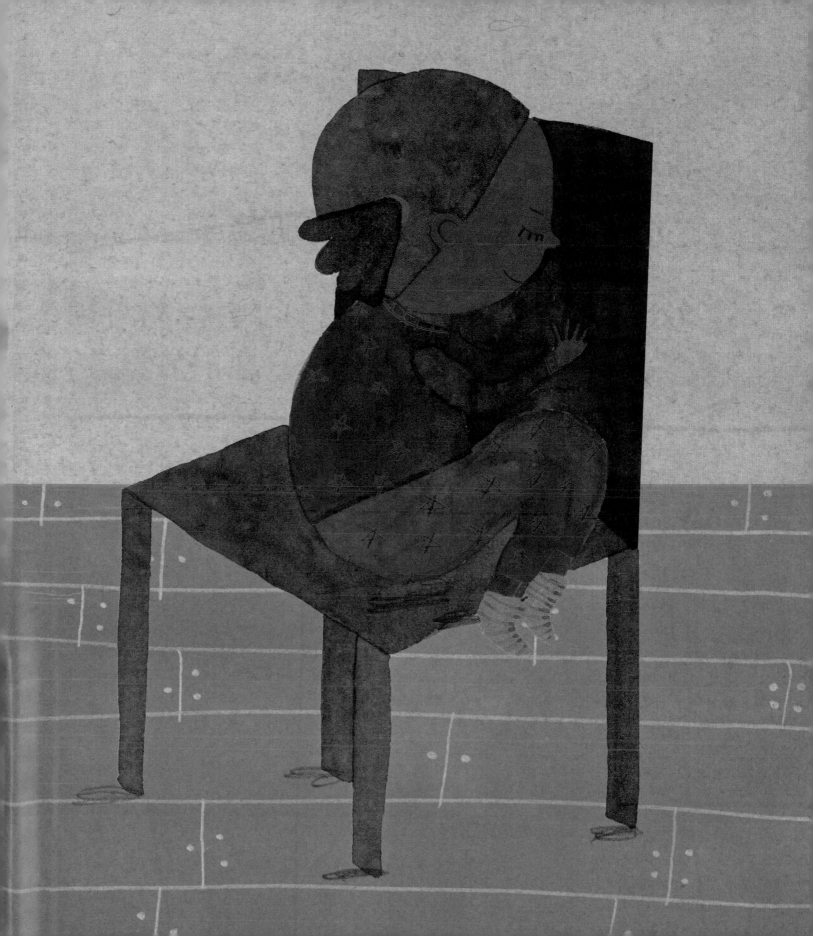